T0353737

Adam & Eve

&

Heart Energy

You have Absolutely and Completely
Everything that You need Inside of You

Christine Kowal

Text, Artwork and Audio copyright © 2014 Christine Kowal

www.ChristineKowal.ca

Balboa Press books may be ordered through booksellers or by contacting:

Balboa Press
A Division of Hay House
1663 Liberty Drive
Bloomington, IN 47403
www.balboapress.com
1 (877) 407-4847

ISBN: 978-1-5043-2727-5 (sc)
ISBN: 978-1-5043-2728-2 (e)

Library of Congress Control Number: 2015901330

Print information available on the last page.

Balboa Press rev. date: 10/20/2015

BALBOA.
PRESS
A DIVISION OF HAY HOUSE

Also Available

The Heart Energy Program ~ Let us Begin CD ~ download or hardcopy

Adam & Eve & Heart Energy audio book ~ download

Adam & Eve & Heart Energy High Quality Art Prints

at

www.ChristineKowal.ca

This book is dedicated to Nelson Mandela and Dr. Wayne Dyer

The drawings of the light skinned Eve and dark skinned Adam were created in 2014 in honor of Nelson Mandela (1918 - 2013) And all of us who understand that we are all Love inside and that we are All One. You have within you the power to create your world. "You have absolutely and Completely Everything that You need inside of You"

I discovered the words for the drawing of the light skinned Eve and dark skinned Adam "Be still and know I am God" as the main text in a book, recommended by Dr. Wayne Dyer (1940 – 2015) while I was studying his teachings. Dr. Wayne Dyer believed that we are Divine Love/God inside, we are all powerful and we are all connected.

Nelson Mandela and Dr. Wayne Dyer although having disparately different lives, both lived their beliefs, and taught them to the world. We are God/ Divine Love inside, we are all powerful and we are all one.

A piece of God, Light, Love, Universe, Creator is shining
inside of You. "Be Still and Know I Am God"

'The Impersonal Life'

by Joseph S. Benner

Preface

You have to listen to that piece of God/Love/Universe/Creator inside of you, that is your inner guidance system. That is God/Love/Universe/Creator inside of You connected to the God/Love/Universe/Creator outside of You, of All.

And then You have to feel good. When you are happy and you feel good, good things happen, that is simply the Law of Attraction.

Many years ago I drew a book which I called 'My Adam and Eve Book'. It is the story of Genesis as I understand it. My version is a beautiful story, it is the story of life. Getting thrown out of the garden was simply the journey from innocence into adulthood.

One of my favorite things in the world is walking holding hands with the man that I love. And it doesn't really matter how I am feeling once we join hands I feel good. We all need to do things that make us feel good. When we do things that make us feel good, good things happen to us.

All of Our Love Christine and The Animals

Prologue

My Adam and Eve book is a story about God and Love. As I have always understood it Adam and Eve left the Garden because they had to. The eating of the Apple, the shiny red fruit from the Tree of Knowledge was actually them coming into their own. The Transition of their bodies from child to young adult, what North American society calls puberty and the leaving of the Garden was merely Adam and Eve setting out on a new and exciting journey called Life.

The simple pleasures of childhood could no longer hold their attention once they had tasted of one another and they wanted to do it their way, see the world, experience life.

And when they left the Garden of Eden they took God with them, he came inside of them. Because each and every one of us has a piece of God/Love/Universe/Creator inside of us, our own internal guidance system.

And they were now able as adults whose bodies had become mature to experience life fully and share each other with one another. One of the ways you get to experience God is by being with or loving the one you love with your body, that union, that explosion is both of you connecting to God, it is a holy experience and one that takes us out of our bodies temporarily and allows us to feel a little bit like Gods, It is an experience from within.

And through their journey of Life Adam and Eve have a lot of Holy experiences as all loving couples should.

Always choose Love And then go home and make Love.

God is with you and inside of You every step of the way. I hope that you enjoy our story. We believe it will make you feel good and it will make you go home and be with the one that You Love.

Part 1 ~ In The Beginning

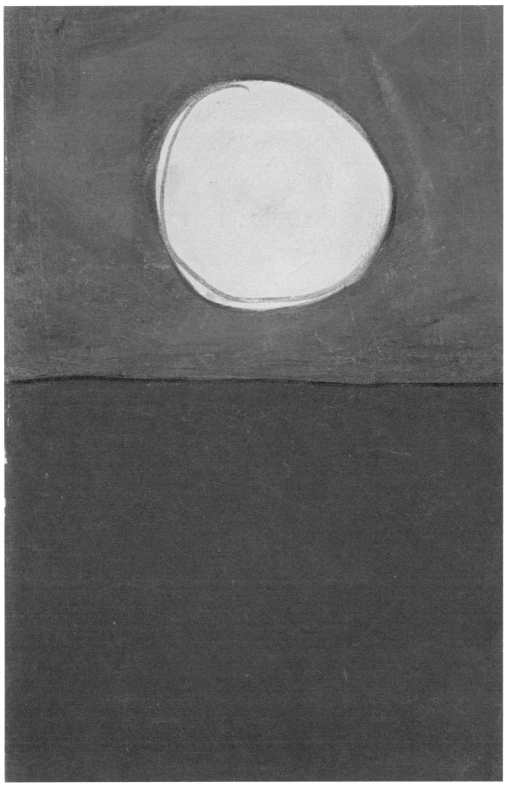

"In the beginning God Created the Heaven and The Earth". "And
God said Let their be Light and there was light."

'The Holy Bible' - Genesis Chapter 1(pg. 3)

God separated the land with waters and this was good.

God created the sea creatures and the birds that flew in the sky.

God created the children that grew out of the earth, the trees and the plants and all the natural vegetation and he saw that this was good.

God created light and day and day and night. The day was when there was sunshine and the sky was bright it was a time for growth and productivity when everyone shared and loved with one another. The night when the moon was out and the sky was dark and black was a time of rest and love and rejuvenation for all. And both the light and the dark were very beautiful and special in their own way.

God created the land animals in male and female form so that they could roam the land and procreate and the land became full and happy as was the sky and the water and God saw that this was good.

God wanted someone to care for the Earth and all of its Children and so God created Man. God made man from the Earth in his image and he saw that this was good.

Man asked God for a mate, a friend, someone like himself who would make him feel good and bring him joy and he in turn would do the same for her. He saw that God had created mates in the animal world and the sea world and the plant world and the sky world and he wanted this kind of relationship for himself. Someone that he could play with and they could explore this new world that God had created together and so God made Eve.

Now it is said that God created Eve from man's rib and as man was created from the Earth we could say that Eve was created from man's rib via the Earth. I don't think that we should worry about this part to much, I know I have thought about it over the years over and over again and I don't think it much matters because we are All Love and Light inside.

From the Beginning Adam and Eve felt right together and off they went to explore the Garden, and God saw that his creations were happy and good and so he decided that a little rest and celebration was in order and so God created Sunday. Sunday is the day that many celebrate God and life and various other landmarks and ceremonies in their lives, and it is also known as the day of rest for that is the day that God rested.

And those of us who have children human or fury know that when you take your attention away from your children they will find something new to play with.

And so Adam and Eve found the 'Tree of Life' now God had told them about the tree of Life. God had told Adam and Eve should they eat the fruit from the Tree of Life, the Apple, their eyes would be opened, meaning the understanding that they would have after they had tasted the fruit from the tree would change them forever and they would never be able to go back to the innocence that they new before.

Well as Adam and Eve wondered over to the Tree of Life, they met the snake who sat up high in the tree next to the beautiful red fruit, the Apple.

Now the snake was a different type of land creature from any that they new, the snake was a reptile and the snake used his entire body to feel and look into and understand the Earth and its Children. So the snake had a very deep and great understanding of each and everything that it moved across.

And the Snake wanted Adam and Eve to understand how absolutely and completely wonderful this new understanding that they would have of each other and the world would be were they to eat the beautiful red fruit, the Apple, from the Tree of Life.

The fruit was high up in the tree and so Eve reached up but could not get to it.

Then Adam reached for the fruit but he also could not access it.

Eve was determined to get to the fruit, she loved what the snake had told her and she had decided that she wanted the understanding for herself and her mate Adam, so she focused, raised herself up on her toes, saw and felt herself plucking the Apple from the tree, determined that the Apple would be theirs, Eve touched the apple and then plucked it from the tree.

She took a bite

And then before she could determine any changes in how she felt, she reached the Apple up to Adam's mouth and gave him a bite too. And so their adventure began.

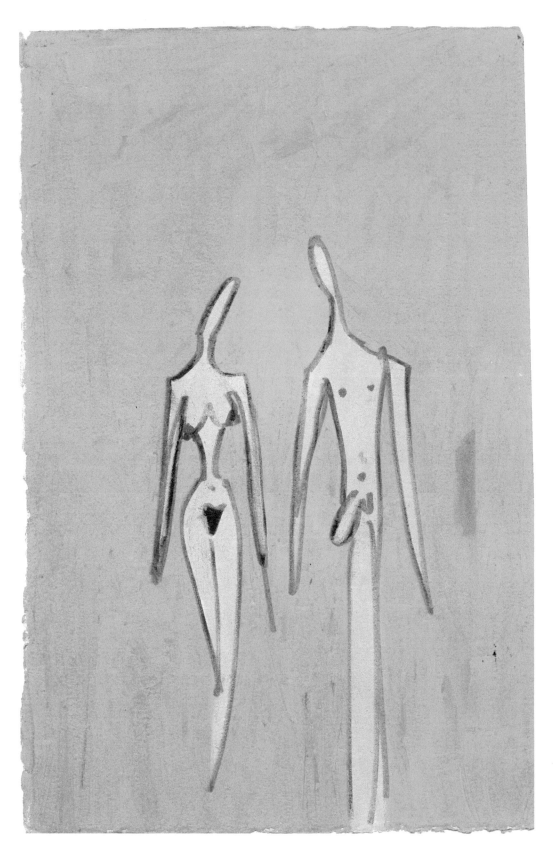

After they had taken a bite of the Apple they looked down at one another and saw each other in a different way. Now when they looked upon one another they felt a hunger for each other that they had not felt before.

This was new to them and so Adam reached over and touched
Eve on the thatch of hair between her legs.

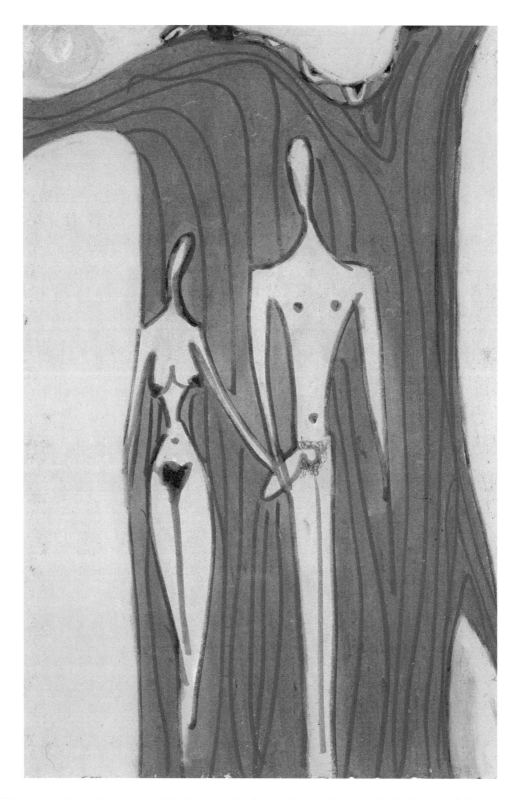

Eve felt a longing rise up within her as she looked at Adam and the beautiful appendage that grew from a thatch of hair between Adam's legs and when she touched it she felt it spring to life and she felt Adam tense and her own body responded with an intensified moisture between her legs which had began when Adam had first touched her.

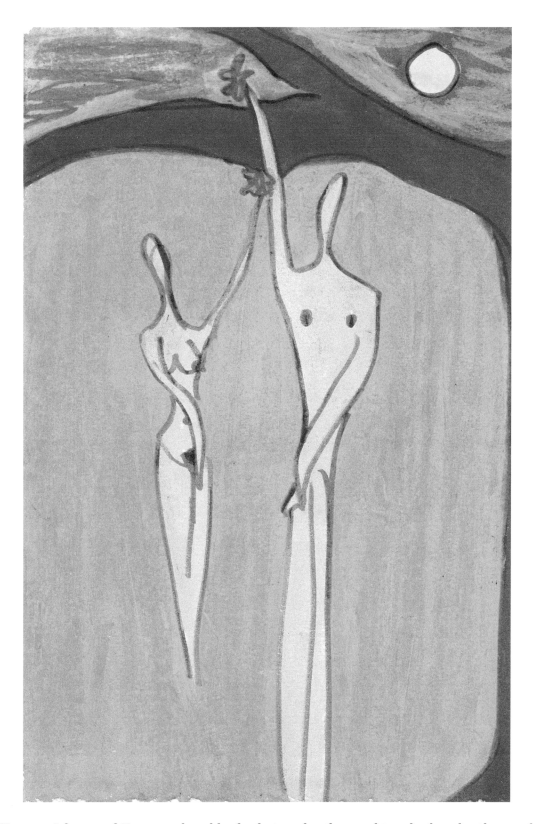

Now as Adam and Eve stood and looked at each other and touched each other and felt these new feelings and yearnings and had these new thoughts they understood that they would now have to cover up those parts on their bodies that created such a yearning for one another. Otherwise they would be able to think of nothing else, and so they created fig coverings for their beautiful places on their bodies.

And they saw that the fig leaf coverings were good and that they worked a little bit.

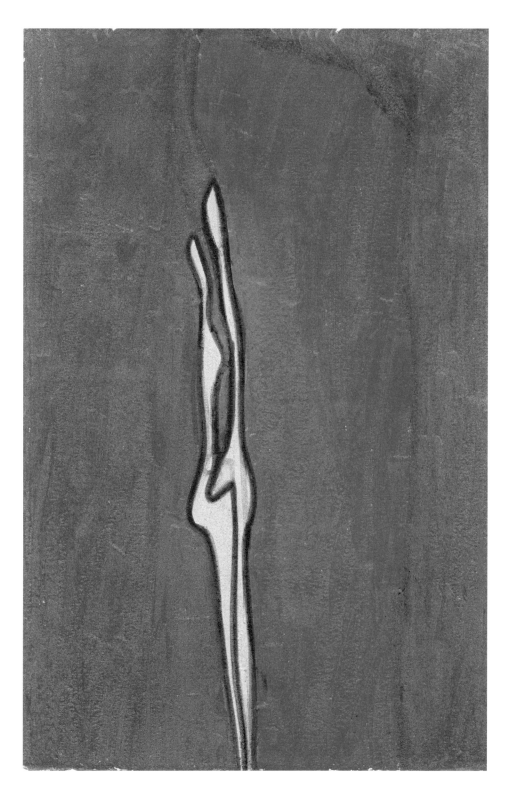

But now that they had this knowledge and understanding of one another they wanted to be closer to one another all of the time. Once they had felt that feeling of union, that oneness, once Adam was inside of Eve, they both new that they would want this for the rest of their lives, they could never go back to the innocence before they had eaten the shiny red fruit, the apple, from the tree of life and tasted of one another, just as the wise snake had told them.

Part 2 ~ Getting Thrown Out of The Garden

And so God spoke with them and explained, now that they had tasted of one another their understanding of life had altered and he clothed them and sent them out into the world to learn and understand and appreciate the beauty of one another and the whole world. It was their time to leave the sheltered Garden and set out on The Joyous Adventure of Their Lives. God would always be inside of them, guiding their way.

Now although Adam and Eve no longer lived in Gods sheltered Garden
they had a piece of God inside of them so he was always with them. Their
inner guidance system made their outward journey clear to them.

Although they did not always understand why their inner guidance system was telling
them to do certain things. They soon learned to understand that their inner guidance
system, their gut feeling was their connection with God and when they followed
it all was well and when they didn't follow it, when they did something that didn't
feel right from the inside then nothing turned out quite the way that it should.

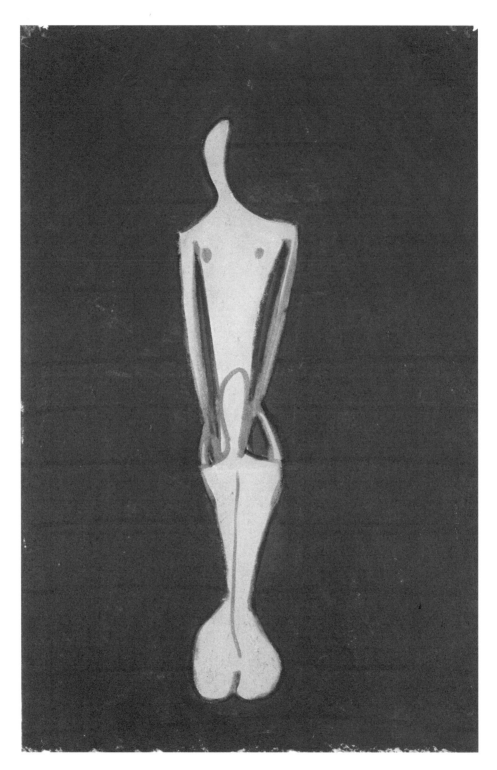

One of the most wonderful gifts that God have given them was their ability and joy in sharing one an others bodies with each other. They explored each other in many many different ways working at making each other feel good and in doing so creating this incredible feeling of oneness that they felt body mind and spirit within their core. And this particular feeling was only possible when they were together loving one another.

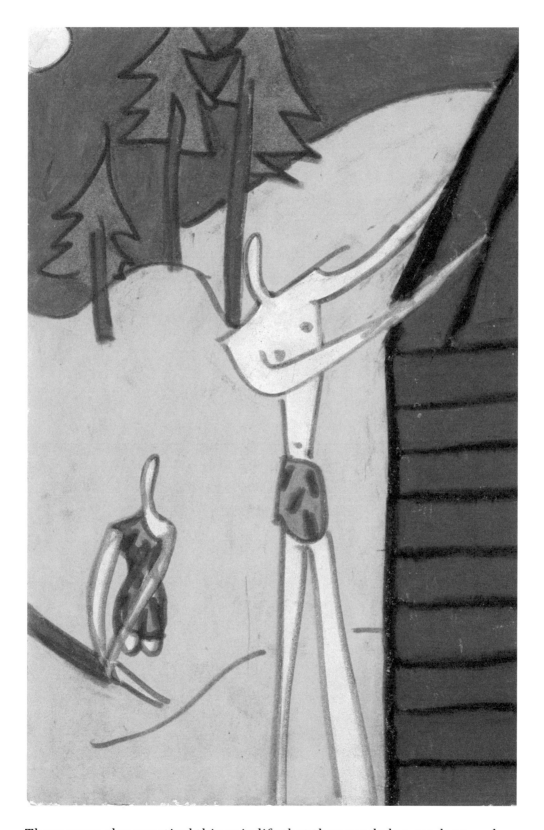

There were also practical things in life that they needed to get done such as shelter. When they had been living in the Garden of Eden, everything had been provided for them, now they needed to create these things for themselves.

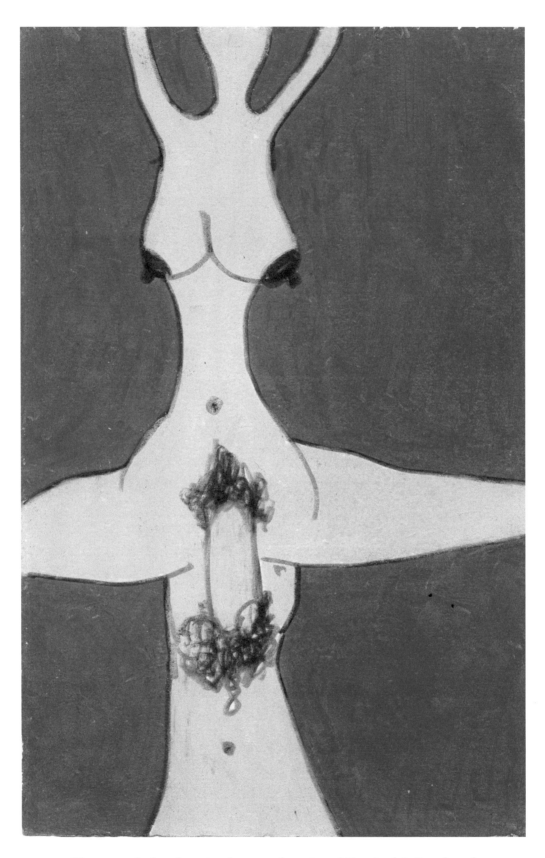

They needed a place to sleep and rest and Be. And A Good and
Safe place to explore one another. For exploring one another had
become a Wonderful and Important part of their lives.

One of their favorite things was going for a walk together and holding hands.

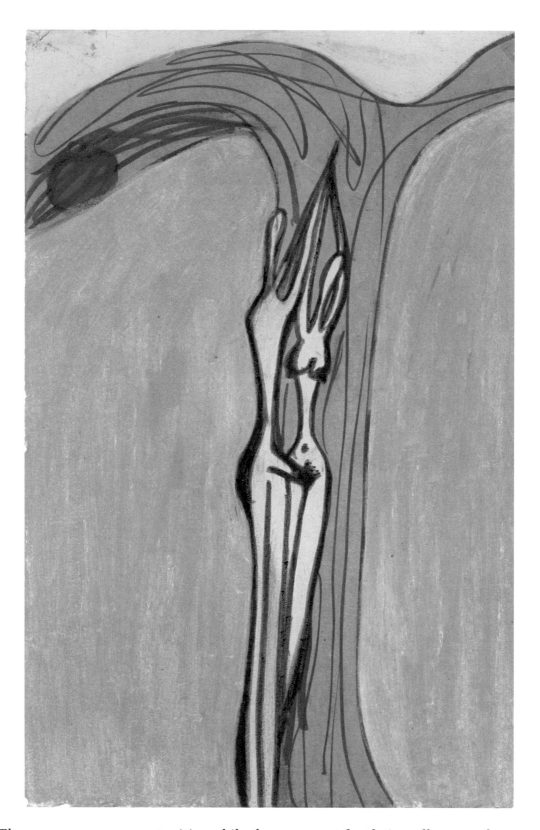

There were many opportunities while they were out for their walks to explore one another and while out for their walk one day they found a tree that was similar to The Tree of Life, it bore the beautiful red fruit the snake had called the Apple and so they felt compelled to Christen the tree with the knowledge it had given them in thanks.

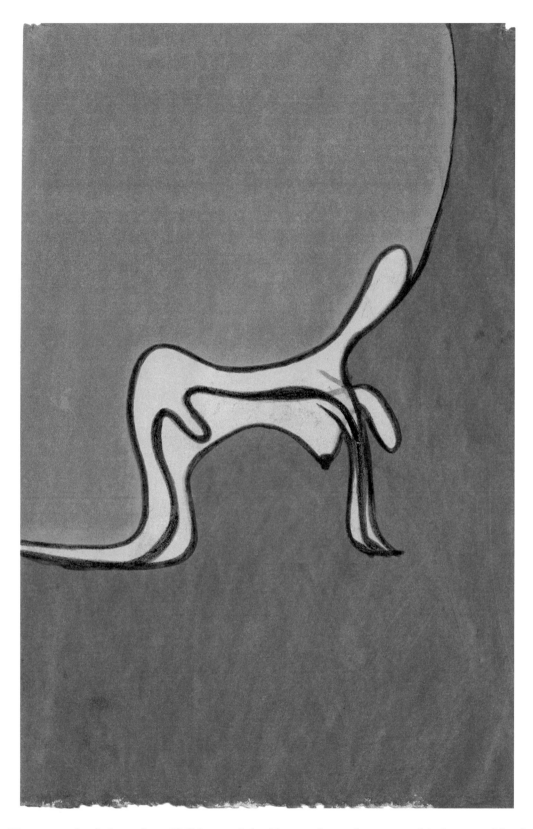

They watched the other Children of the Forest, how they mated in love and had fun together without any hesitation, and they did the same. When one would catch the others attention in a gesture or body position and that yearning would well up inside of them, they would fall upon one another until they were both satiated.

They followed their inner knowing, that piece of God inside of them and they
new that if it felt right and good to both of them then it was good.

They learnt that different seasons required that they do different things. When the plants were growing and plentiful they gathered enough to eat, and enough for later when the ground was not so plentiful.

And they found many places and new ways of positioning one and other amongst and upon the trees that brought pleasure to both of them.

The cold months were coming and the forest where they lived had turned to red and gold.
They prepared for the long winter months when they would spend much of their time
indoors. They gathered wood for the fire and nuts for their winter stores as they prepared.

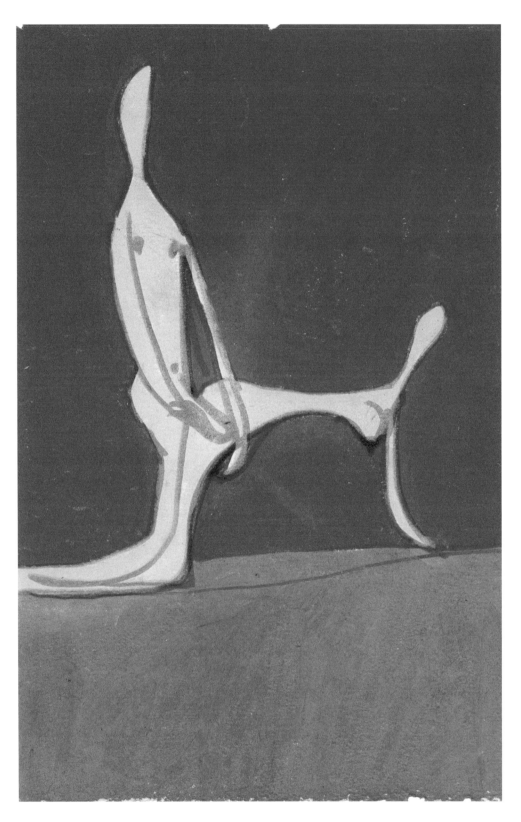

And as the winter months came about they were able to spend more time indoors exploring one another. They remembered what they had learnt from the other children of the Earth and now they created different variations for themselves. Adam always working towards pleasing Eve, and Eve always working towards pleasing Adam.

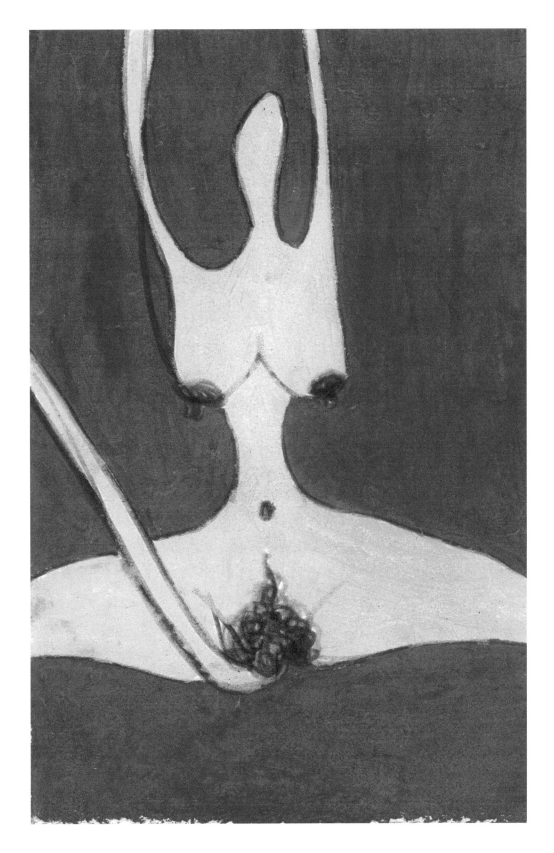

Exploring one an others preferences and teaching each other about who they each were and what made them both happy or incredibly excited was a wonderful thing.

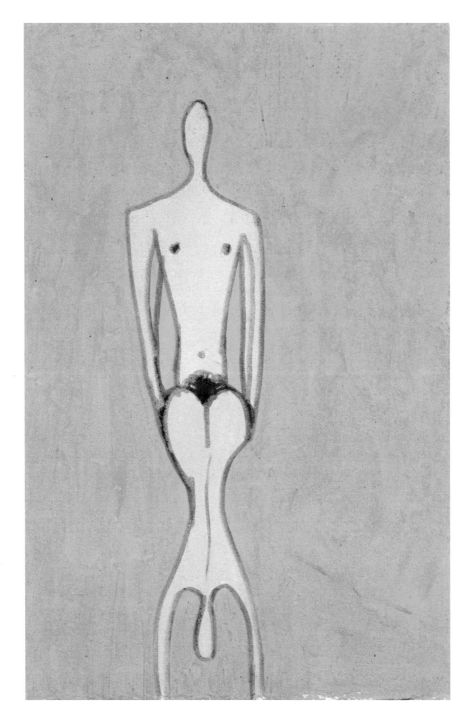

And their were many new ways to love one another that they learned and explored as the winter months kept them indoors. They now understood when God and the snake had told them that once they ate the fruit from the tree of Life, the Apple, they could not go back to their innocence.

Now that they understood how loving one another with mind body and spirit made them feel and how it felt when they orgasmed together, they understood that this was one of the most beautiful ways to experience God together as one, it took them to a place they could not reach on their own. And they understood that this was good and this was God and this was Love when two became One.

There were other things that they enjoyed together through the long winter months. The warm wooly clothing that they had fashioned in the style of the clothes that God had first given them when they left the garden. The hot fire in the fire chamber that Adam had fashioned from the colored stones that they had found in the water, kept their home warm and safe.

Now that they were home together and spent so much time indoors they started experimenting with each others bodies thoughts and feelings and they found new and interesting positions and ways of placing their bodies that pleasured both of them.

Winter turned to spring and they found themselves outside in the fresh new world again. Although they had enjoyed the long winter months indoors enjoying one another, it was wonderful to be outside in the fresh spring air with the snow melting into the river and the trees and plants poking their heads up out of the soil.

It seemed that the more time Adam spent inside of Eve

And the more time they spent together, inside, around and rubbing up against one another the closer they felt to each other and the greater their hunger became for one another.

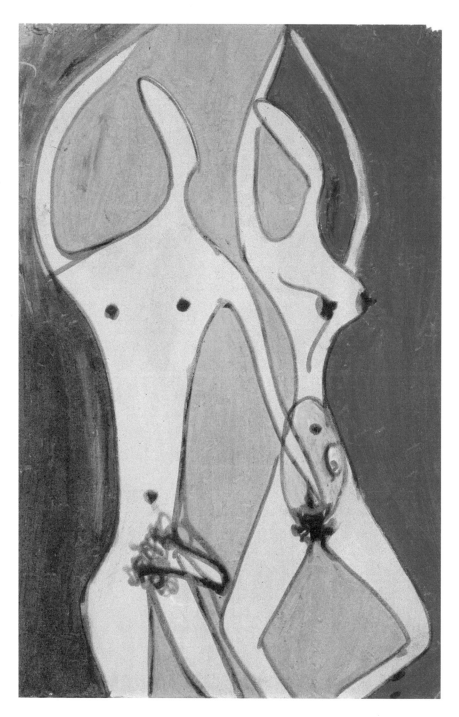

And then one day while Adam was playing with Eve she felt something
new inside of her tummy but she didn't quite know what it was.

Now although Adam and Eve no longer lived in the Garden of Eden and didn't see God in
the way that they used to see him, they continued to visit with him. But they no longer had
to see him to speak with him, they just had to close their eyes, put their hands on their
heart and ask him a question or call to him and he would be there, inside of them, right
behind their Heart, their inner knowing, their Heart Energy communicating with them.
God had come with them. There was a piece of God inside each of them that they could
call upon for advice whenever it was needed or when they just wanted to talk to God.

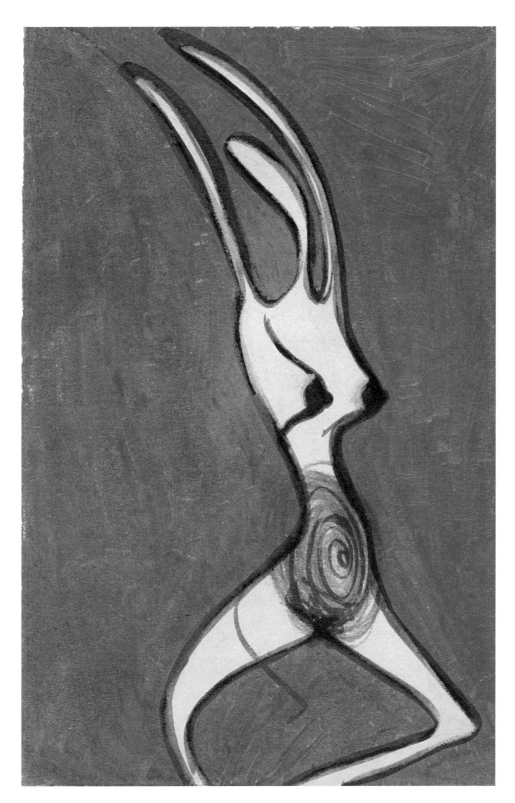

When Eve lay down and closed her eyes she felt that strange feeling in her tummy which seemed to be getting bigger every day and she asked God what was happening.

And God said that she was going to have a baby just like she'd seen the animals and the other children of the Earth giving birth, it was now Eve's and Adam's time to have a baby, one of their own.

And not to worry about the changes in her body, they were normal as she grew their baby inside of her. Her breasts became larger and more tender, her belly got bigger because this is where God said their baby was growing and she felt that hunger growing inside of her that needed satisfying more and more often, and so she began learning how to pleasure herself as Adam had pleasured her many times before.

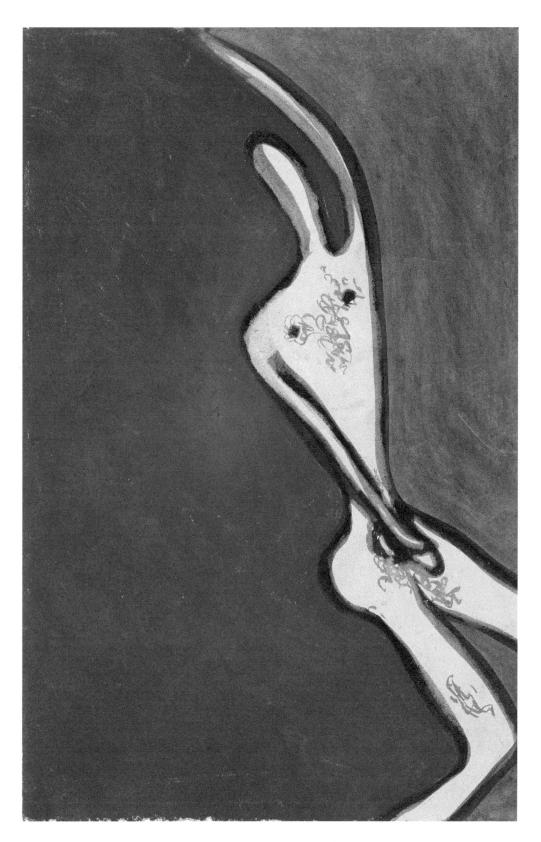

They both started to enjoy this new way of playing with one another. They would pleasure themselves and the other would watch. It felt daring and new and exciting for both of them.

Something that they still both enjoyed and had learned together in the Garden of Eden, one of their most favorite things to do, was hold hands and go for long walks together.

Eve found that this was very important to her and the baby as their bodies grew and were changing together, God had told them that it was very important for them to walk so Adam and Eve and Baby inside, went on many wonderful long walks together in the forest by their new home.

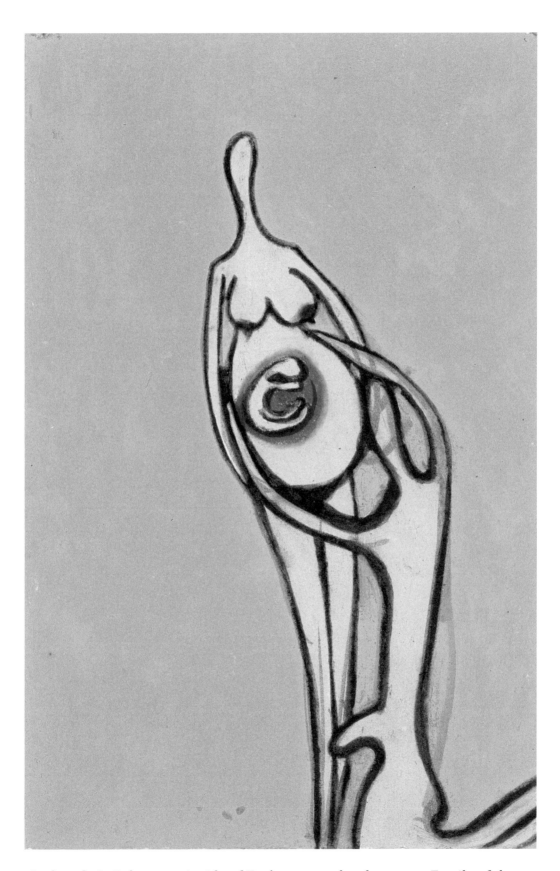

And as their Baby grew inside of Eve's tummy they became a Family of three.

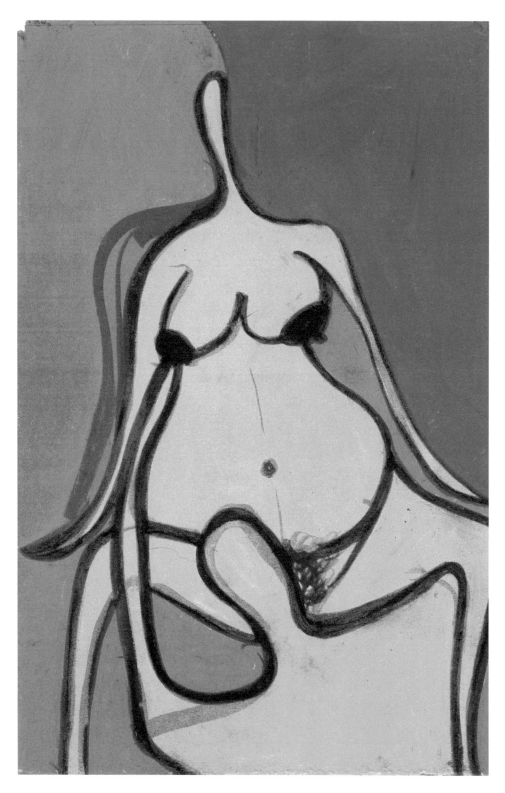

They continued to find ways to please one another. It was not always easy to find a good position for both of them to feel good, as Eve's body grew and changed to accommodate their growing baby inside, but they were relentless in their pursuit of pleasing one another.

That bond that they had formed so long ago when their eyes were first opened in the Garden of Eden, when they had really seen each other for the first time in their fullness, continued to grow stronger.

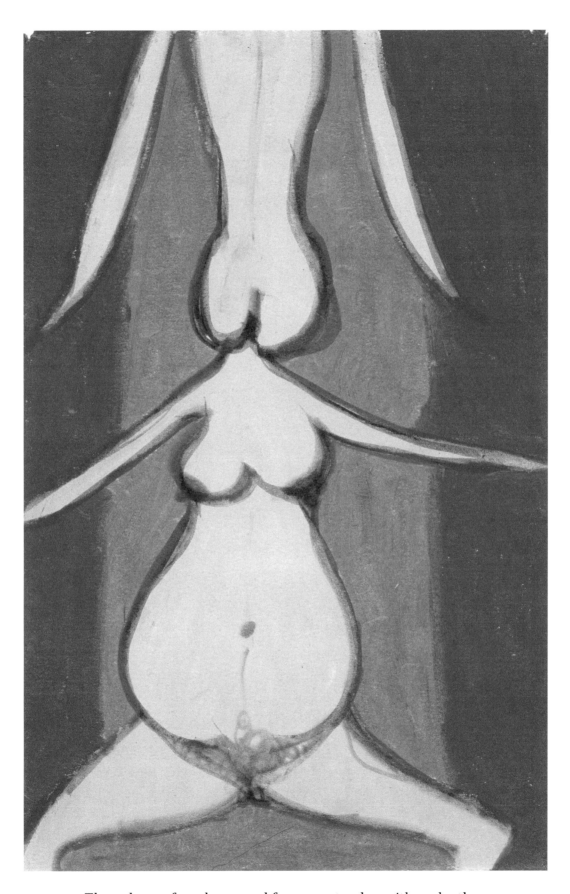

They always found new and fun ways to play with each other.

And as Eve's time drew nearer their walks increased. God said to them that they must walk more now as the time drew nearer, it would make it easier for both Eve and the baby, and he told them that he would be there for them when the time came and all was well.

Part 3 ~ The Miracle of Life

Eve could never have imagined what she would have to go through to bring their baby out into the world. However God had told her to remain standing like she had seen the animals do, and to only sit when she needed to take a break. And Adam was their by her side helping in every way that he could and God was also there with them, directing them and helping in the natural unfolding of events. Although they could not see God they could feel him in their hearts and by their side.

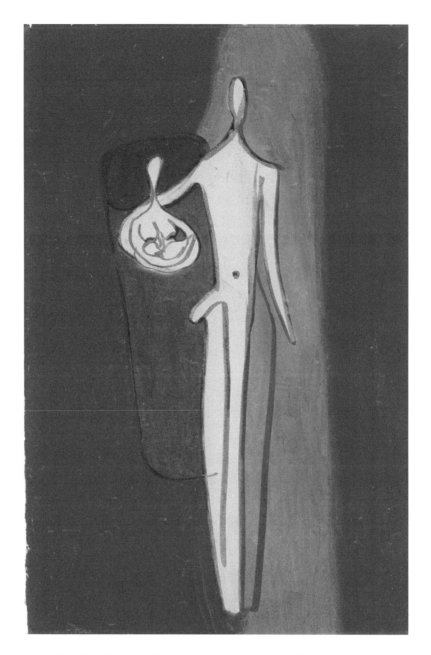

And so Adam and Eve had trusted God when he had told them, that now that they had the knowledge of one another they would no longer be happy living in the Garden of Eden with him. They had to go out into the world and find their own happiness. He told them that he was always inside of them and outside of them protecting them and showing them the way and now they understood a little more. And they new that their new baby, Young Adam, would always walk with God as well, and this was good.

They had this brand new baby, a tiny little version of themselves, more like Adam of course than Eve for he was a boy. And they were now a family, Adam and Eve, Young Adam and God inside and by their side.

And God assured them that the next part of their journey would be just as wonderful as the first had been. They had learned to believe in themselves, to trust God, their higher power from within and to trust and believe in one another and all was well.

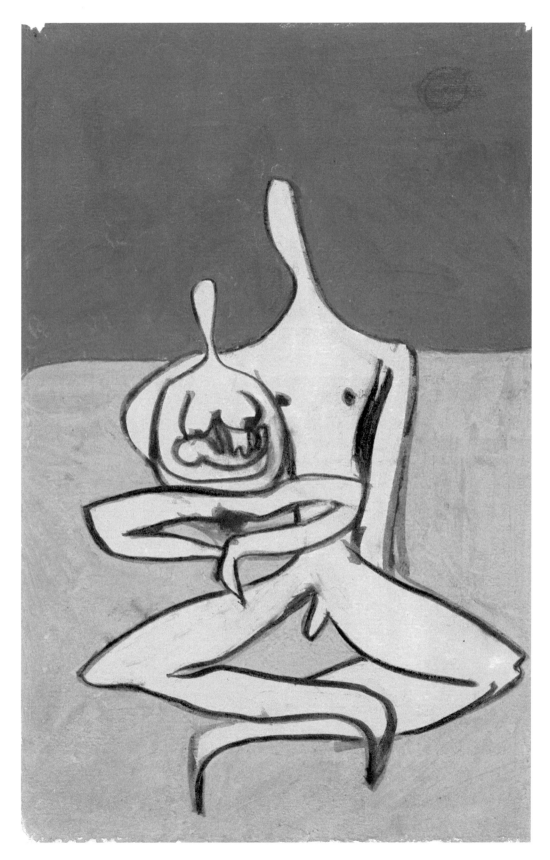

Raising a child together was a whole new world. Sometimes if felt
like the most natural thing in the world, and at other times they
didn't know if what they were doing was the right thing.

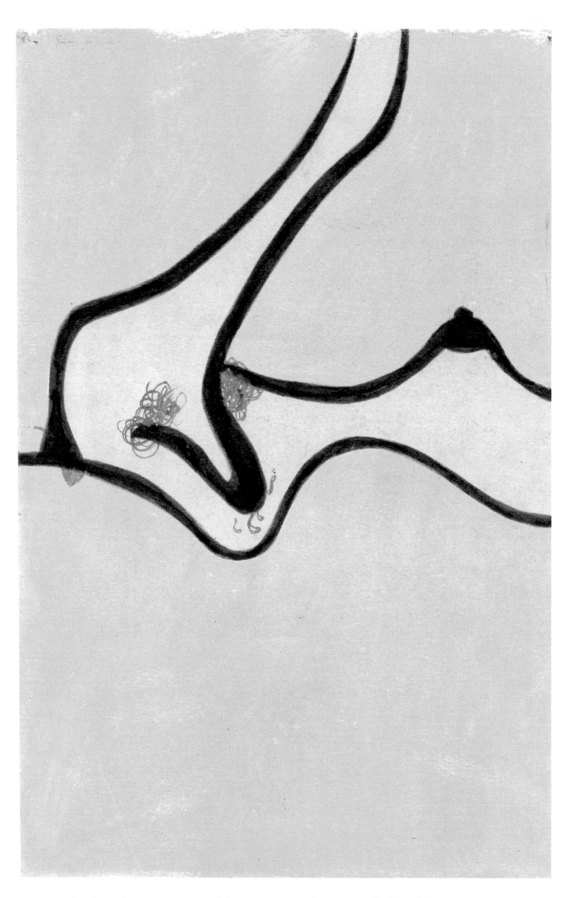

And so the next part of their journey began and they felt stronger
together and more as one than they had ever felt before.

And each and every time seemed to feel better than the last. It didn't matter why, all that mattered was that Adam be inside of Eve and Eve engulf Adam from within.

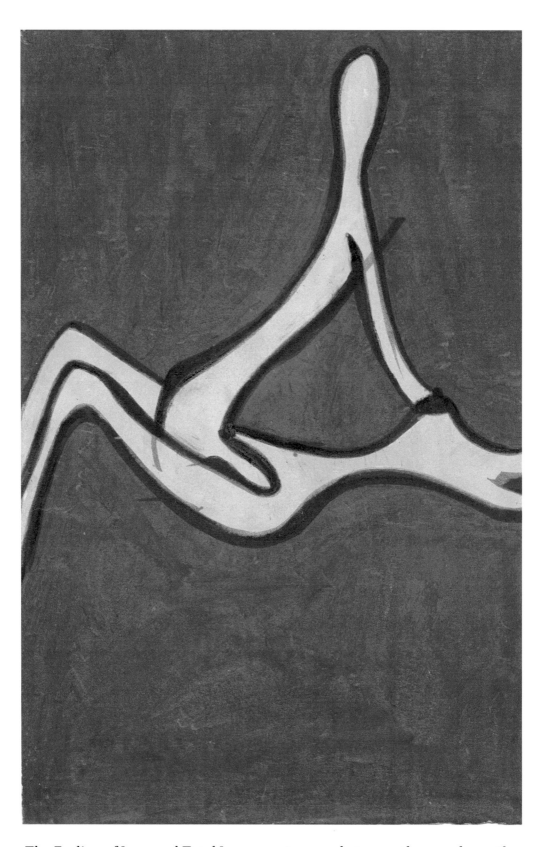

The Feeling of Love and Total Joy grew stronger between them and was the most powerful when Adam was inside of Eve, it was a place they reached together like nothing else in the world. For them it was like the joining of that piece of God inside of them. It was a holy collision of body mind and spirit.

And they were now a family of three plus God. They belonged to one another
and their little boy belonged to both of them and they belonged to him.

And as he grew they tried to teach him everything that they could remember learning in the Garden of Eden, when they lived in that innocent time with God, when they could actually see God in their child like innocence. Before they ate of the Apple, the red fruit from The Tree of Knowledge and their yearning for one another took over their mind body and spirit.

And they did their best, and they new that God was with them guiding their son as he had guided them when they were young, and all was well.

And they new that one day soon their son would find his own Young Eve and then he would get to experience the knowledge and understanding of Loving another with one's body mind and spirit. And they were Happy for him, for this was one of the greatest gifts that God had given them. And they understood now why this knowledge had not come at first but at just the right time.

Young Adam had met a girl over in the next forest and her name was Young Eve and they often played together and sometimes they watched what his parents were doing. And as Young Adam and Young Eve got older sometimes new and exciting feelings and thoughts would come into their heads and take over their body mind and spirit and they would feel a strange tugging and pulling and yearning towards one another and if felt good, it felt Very Good.

And then one day Young Adam found himself sitting under an apple tree with his friend, Young Eve, she felt different and she smelt different to him and he felt that yearning start up inside of him. He had spoken to God about it earlier that day and God had been explaining things to him as he felt the changes in his body and he new that all was well.

Young Adam had been Young Eve's friend forever but somehow, now he felt and looked different to her. He was so beautiful and she new that she wanted to taste Adam, she wanted to kiss him. She had been talking to God about it for quite some time now and God had told her that when the time was right, a snake would appear to them in the Apple tree and that would be their sign. And now there was a snake up in the apple tree under which they sat.

Young Eve and Young Adam were excited about what God had told them and they new that once they tasted of one another their world would be changed forever into an even more bright and beautiful world than they could possibly imagine.

Once they tasted of one another they would know God differently, he would from then on live inside of them and they would no longer be children. He had told them that instead of him appearing next to them like a friend he would live inside of them from then on, right behind their Heart and he would communicate to them through their Heart Energy, that piece of God inside of them, their place of inner knowing. He would from then on be their guidance system from within.

And that the feelings that Young Adam and Young Eve would have for one another would be so powerful and overwhelming that it was best that they now kept God, their guidance system inside of them for that is where all of the important feelings would now be coming from.

And they new that all was well, they could feel it.

The Heart Energy Prayer/Meditation

I have Absolutely and Completely Everything that I need inside of me, and I am free and I am safe and I am whole and I am strong and I am prosperous and I Love myself and I am Light

and Breathe

I have Absolutely and Completely Everything that I need inside of me, and I am free and I am safe and I am whole and I am strong and I am prosperous and I Love myself and I am Light

and Breathe

I have Absolutely and Completely Everything that I need inside of me, and I am free and I am safe and I am whole and I am strong and I am prosperous and I Love myself and I am Light

and Breathe

Epilogue

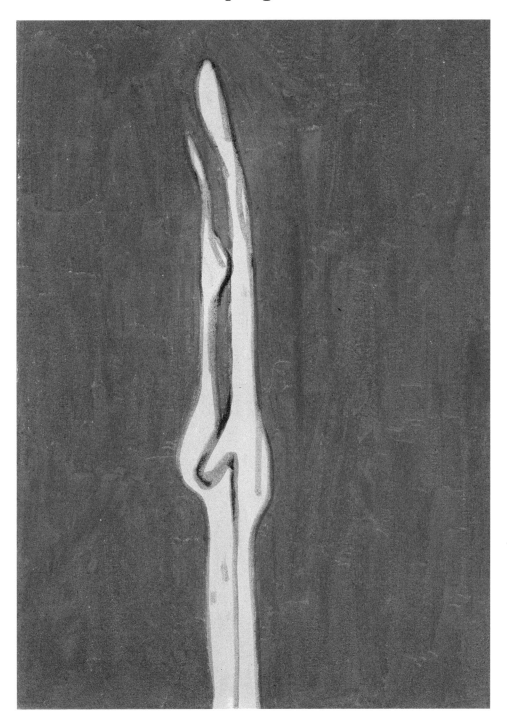

Empowerment is following your inner guidance system, that piece of God/Love/
Universe/Creator inside of You, your gut feeling, in each and every decision
that you make and remembering to do what you love each and every day
over and over again. Always Choose Love And then go home and make Love
"Absolutely and Completely Everything that You need is Inside of You"

Printed in the United States
By Bookmasters